988p

Educational Adviser: Lynda Snowdon
Designer: Julian Holland
Picture researcher: Stella Martin
Artist for Contents pages: Julian Holland

Photo credits:
J. Allan Cash, 16-17, 22-23, 28-29; Aspect
Picture Library, 12-13; Alan Hutchison
Library, 8-11, 20-21, 26-27; Stella Martin, 30-31;
Sally and Richard Greenhill, 24-25; ZEFA, 4-7, 14-15, 18-19
Cover picture: Aspect Picture Library

Dillon Press, Inc., 242 Portland Avenue South
Minneapolis, Minnesota 55415

This edition published by Dillon Press by arrangement
with Macmillan Children's Books, London, England.
© Macmillan Publishers Limited, 1983

Library of Congress Cataloging-in-Publication Data

Perham, Molly.
  People at work.

  (International picture library)
  Summary: Text and photographs describe various jobs
performed by people around the world, including nursing,
fishing, sheep farming, film-making, and fire fighting.
  1. Occupations — Juvenile literature.
[1. Occupations]   I. Title.   II. Series.
HF5382.P47   1986   331.7'02   86-2014
ISBN 0-87518-333-6

International Picture Library

People At Work

Molly Perham

DILLON PRESS, INC.
Minneapolis, Minnesota 55415

Contents

10   Cutting Sugar-Cane in Barbados

4   Fishing in Mexico

12   Drilling for Oil in Mexico

6   Sheepfarming in Australia

14   A Market in Guatemala

8   Planting Rice in Malaysia

16   Breadmaking in England

18   Making Pots in Nepal

20   A Village Clinic in Zaire

22   Firefighters in Action in Canada

24   Primary Schoolteacher in England

26   Policeman Directing Traffic in India

28   Filming in Nigeria

30   Working in an Office, London, England

32   Places Featured in this Book

Fishing in Mexico

These Mexican fishermen are using special nets
which are shaped like butterflies. The fishermen
hold the poles between the "wings." They slide the

nets under the fish to catch them. The fishing boats are very small and made of wood. The fisherman moves the boat slowly through the water with a paddle.

Sheepfarming in Australia

Australia has more sheep than any other country in
the world. Sheep stations (ranches) there are very large.
The farmers raise sheep for their wool and their meat.

These sheep are being rounded up. It is time to have their woolly coats cut. This is called shearing. The wool will be spun and woven into cloth. Much of the cloth is sold to people in other countries.

Planting Rice in Malaysia
Rice is the main food for half the people in the
world. These women in Malaysia are planting
seedlings in a paddy field. They are wading

barefoot in the mud. Their big hats shade them from the hot sun. The plants need plenty of water. If there is no rain the rice will not grow, and millions of people will not have enough to eat.

Cutting Sugar-Cane in Barbados
A lot of the sugar that we eat comes from
sugar-cane. Sugar-cane grows in countries that are
hot and have a lot of rain. The canes can grow to

more than twice the height of a person in one year.
They are cut down and taken to a factory. Then
they are crushed by heavy rollers to squeeze out
the juice. The juice is turned into sugar.

Drilling for Oil in Mexico

These men are drilling a hole to find oil. Oil comes
from deep down inside the earth. If the men are
lucky, they will reach oil underground. The

oil will then come gushing up into the air. Oil is
used in many ways. We need oil as fuel for our
factories and our cars. We also need it to heat
our homes.

A Market in Guatemala

These women have come to the market to sell goods. In Guatemala many of the people live in small villages. They grow their own food. They also

make baskets, pottery and woodcarvings. The
women spin, weave and dye cloth. They make
clothes for themselves and for their families. They
sell the things they do not need themselves.

15

Breadmaking in England

The bread that you buy in a store has probably been made in a bakery or a factory. Machines do most of the work, and people are needed to work the

machines. This bakery assistant is working one
which is rolling out some dough. Another machine
will cut the dough and put the pieces into tins. The
loaves will then be baked in a huge oven.

Making Pots in Nepal

The villagers here make pots from clay. The pots are perfectly round and smooth. They have been made on a potter's wheel. Now, they are being left

out in the sun to dry. When they are dry they will be baked in an oven, or kiln. This will make them hard and able to hold water. The pots will probably be sold in the market.

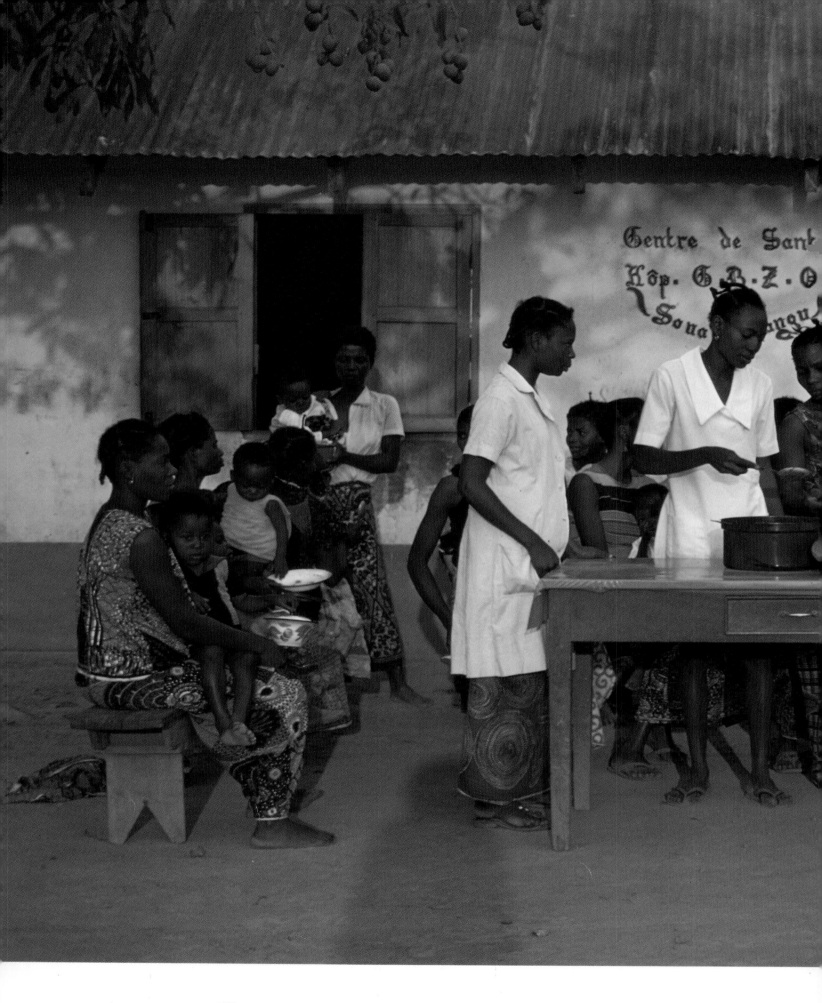

A Village Clinic in Zaire

The doctor and nurses work in Zaire. The village
women bring their children to see the doctor at the
baby clinic. The nurses show them how to feed their

children and keep them clean. They also check that
the children are healthy and tell their mothers the
best food to give them. They may give them shots,
injections, to stop them from getting ill.

Firefighters in Action in Canada
These firefighters are hard at work putting out a fire.
The long hose carries water. The firefighters will
hold the end and squirt water on the flames.

There is a ladder on the fire engine which is used to rescue people from tall buildings. The firefighters have to wear special clothes, and sometimes a mask to help them breathe.

Primary Schoolteacher in England
This teacher is marking the children's work. They have written a story. Each child has chosen one of the titles written up on the blackboard. The walls of

the classroom are covered with work done by the children. Some schoolchildren in England have to wear a uniform to school. These children do not need to.

Policeman Directing Traffic in India

Directing traffic is part of a police officer's job. In India officers direct bullock carts and bicycles as well as cars. Here, the policeman is standing on a

raised platform. The colorful canopy shades him
from the sun. Everyone can see him. If a driver
does something wrong, the policeman will blow a
whistle.

Filming in Nigeria

These men are shooting a film in Nigeria. The cameraman is filming the cattle as they walk out of the water. The camera is on a tripod to keep it

steady. The man in the red hat is the director of the
film. He will choose the best pictures at the end of
the day. He will then put them together to make
the film.

Working in an Office, London, England

Office workers usually sit at desks for most of the
day. This young woman works in an office where
books and magazines are produced. On her desk

are many papers which she has to read. She needs
a quiet room so that she can think. She writes letters
and types them on the typewriter. Sometimes, she
talks on the telephone.

Places Featured in this Book

1	Fishing, Mexico	**8**	Making Pots, Nepal
2	Sheepfarming, Australia	**9**	Village Clinic, Zaire
3	Planting Rice, Malaysia	**10**	Firefighters, Canada
4	Cutting Sugar-Cane, Barbados	**11**	Schoolteacher, England
5	Drilling for Oil, Mexico	**12**	Policeman, India
6	Market, Guatemala	**13**	Filming, Nigeria
7	Breadmaking, England	**14**	Office, London, England